Published in 2018 by Windmill Books,
an Imprint of Rosen Publishing
29 East 21st Street, New York, NY 10010

Copyright © 2018 Blake Publishing

Cover and text design: Leanne Nobilio
Editor: Vanessa Barker

Cataloging-in-Publication Data

Names: Johnson, Rebecca.
Title: Super snakes / Rebecca Johnson.
Description: New York : Windmill Books, 2018. | Series: Reptile
adventures | Includes index.
Identifiers: ISBN 9781508193616 (pbk.) | ISBN 9781508193579
(library bound) | ISBN 9781508193654 (6 pack)
Subjects: LCSH: Snakes—Juvenile literature.
Classification: LCC QL666.O6 J65 2018 | DDC 597.96—dc23

Manufactured in China
CPSIA Compliance Information: Batch BW18WM. For Further Information
contact Rosen Publishing, New York, New York at 1-800-237-9932

REPTILE ADVENTURES

CONTENTS

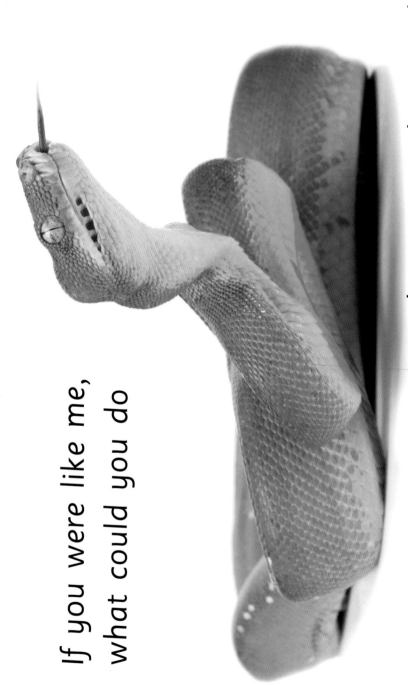

If you were like me,
what could you do

to change people's minds
so they understood you?

Would you hide away and stay out of sight,

just so you wouldn't give people a fright?

3

I know I may scare you
as I slither by,

but I am amazing,
and I'll tell you why.

My tongue is forked,
and I use it to tell
where my prey is hiding.
I need it to smell!

My scales aren't slimy,
but smooth and dry.
Belly scales grip the surface
as I slither on by.

I feel vibrations
come up through the ground.
That's how I know
someone else is around.

I shed my skin
and leave behind
one long piece
for you to find.

Some of us lay eggs, and some are born live.

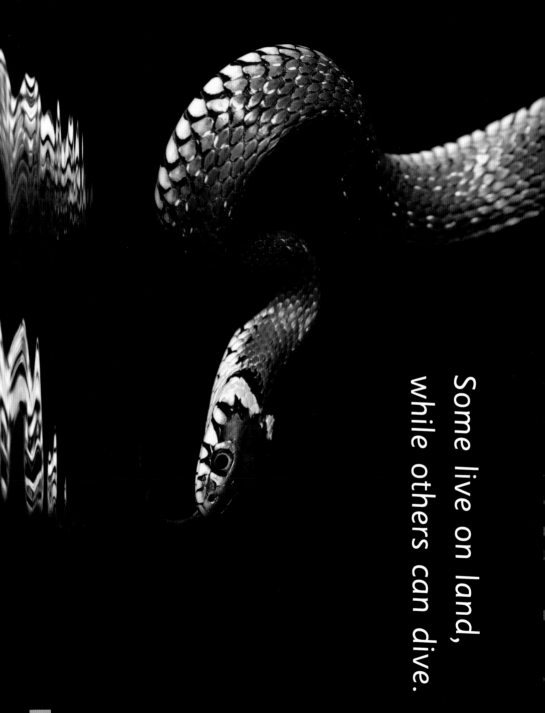

Some live on land, while others can dive.

There are nearly three thousand snake types in the world,

some on the ground, and some in trees, curled.

But of all of these snakes,
there are very few

who would actually choose
to come and bite you.

And while I may bite,
it is often the case . . .

that I'll only do it
if you're giving chase.

All creatures on Earth
are linked in a way....

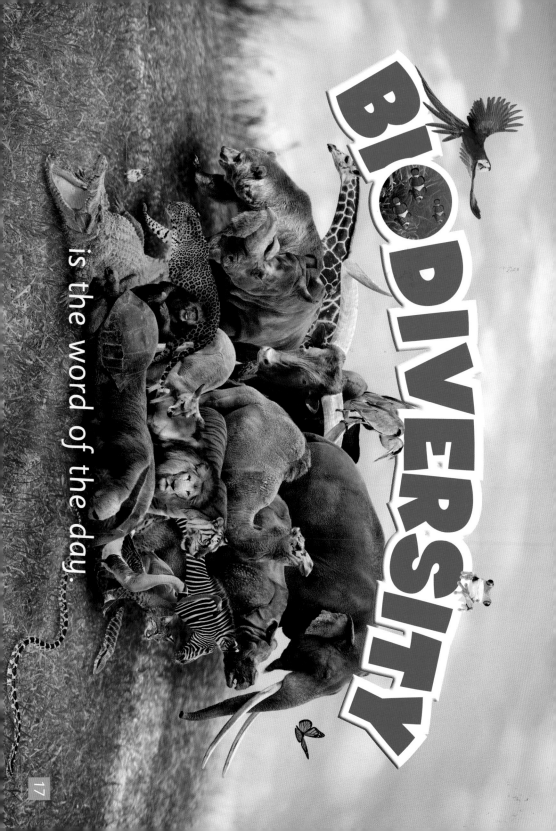

BIODIVERSITY

is the word of the day.

If you take out a link
so there are no snakes,
be prepared for the difference
that action will make.

You see, snakes eat termites and rodents, too.

If we didn't, these pests might invade you.

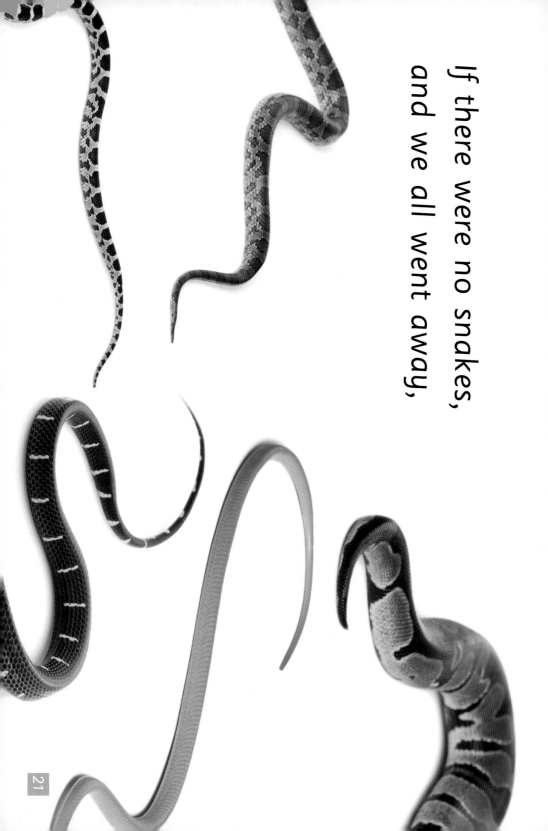

If there were no snakes,
and we all went away,

21

you'd lose other species, like birds of prey.

So now that you've met us,
there's one point worth raising—
you have to agree
that we're pretty amazing!

Reasons Why Snakes Are Good

- Snakes kill rodent pests.
- Snakes eat termites.
- Snakes are part of the food chain.
- Snakes usually only bite if threatened.
- Snakes are food for many native animals.

GLOSSARY

biodiversity the many different plants and animals in an area

birds of prey birds that kill and eat small birds and animals

forked something divided into two parts at one end

linked to be connected

rodents small animals that have sharp front teeth (e.g. mice and rats)

scales small, flat pieces that cover the bodies of fish and reptiles

shed to get rid of or to lose from one's body

slither to slide your body quickly along the ground by twisting

species similar plants or animals that are able to produce young together

vibrations quick and continuous shaking movements